eric

templar *publishing*

ERic

by Shaun Tan

Some years ago we had a foreign exchange student come to live with us. We found it very difficult to pronounce his name correctly, but he didn't mind.

He told us to just call him 'Eric'.

We had repainted the spare room,
bought new rugs and furniture
and generally made sure everything
would be comfortable for him.
So I can't say why it was that Eric
chose to sleep and study most of
the time in our kitchen pantry.

'It must be a cultural thing,' said Mum.
'As long as he is happy.'

We started storing food and kitchen things in other cupboards so we wouldn't disturb him.

But sometimes I wondered if Eric *was* happy; he was so polite that I'm not sure he would have told us if something bothered him.

A few times I saw him through the pantry door gap, studying with silent intensity, and imagined what it might be like for him here in our country.

Secretly I had been looking forward to having a foreign visitor – I had so many things to show him. For once I could be a local expert, a fountain of interesting facts and opinions.

Fortunately, Eric was very curious and always had plenty of questions.

However, they weren't the kind
of questions I had been expecting.

Most of the time I could only say,
'I'm not really sure,' or, 'That's just how
it is.' I didn't feel very helpful at all.

I had planned for us to go on a number of weekly excursions together, as I was determined to show our visitor the best places in the city and its surrounds.

I think Eric enjoyed these trips, but once again, it was hard to really know.

Most of the time Eric seemed
more interested in small things
he discovered on the ground.

I might have found this a little
exasperating, but I kept thinking
about what Mum had said,
about the cultural thing.

Then I didn't mind so much.

Nevertheless, none of us could help but be bewildered by the way Eric left our home: a sudden departure early one morning, with little more than a wave and a polite goodbye.

It actually took us a while to realise
he wasn't coming back.

There was much speculation
over dinner later that evening.
Did Eric seem upset?
Did he enjoy his stay?
Would we ever hear from him again?

An uncomfortable feeling hung in the air, like something unfinished, unresolved. It bothered us for hours, or at least until one of us discovered what was in the pantry.

Go and see for yourself: it's still there after all these years, thriving in the darkness. It's the first thing we show any new visitors to our house. 'Look what our foreign exchange student left for us,' we tell them.

'It must be a cultural thing,' says Mum.

A TEMPLAR BOOK

First published in the UK in 2010 by Templar Publishing,
an imprint of The Templar Company Limited,
The Granary, North Street, Dorking, RH4 1DN, UK
www.templarco.co.uk

The original version of 'Eric' appeared in
'Tales from Outer Suburbia', published in the UK by Templar Publishing
and originally published in Australia by Allen & Unwin
www.allenandunwin.com

10 9 8 7 6 5 4 3 2 1

ISBN 978-1-84877-587-9

Design by Shaun Tan, Inari Kiuru and Bruno Herfst

Printed in China

Australia 2c

www.shauntan.net

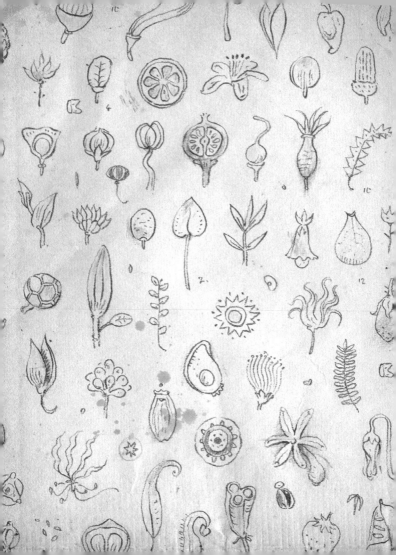